Where do little monsters go to school?
MONSTER ACADEMY

by Jane Yolen and Heidi E. Y. Stemple
illustrated by John McKinley

THE BLUE SKY PRESS
An Imprint of Scholastic Inc. • New York

For our "adopted" grandmonsters—
Julian Harrison Butcher and Sullivan Wilde Schaefer
—J.Y. and H.S.

To Buff, AJ, and Kendra, with love
—J.M.

THE BLUE SKY PRESS

Celebrating 25 Years of Award-winning Publishing

Text copyright © 2018 by Jane Yolen and Heidi E. Y. Stemple
Illustrations copyright © 2018 by John McKinley

Library of Congress catalog card number: 2017032782

ISBN 978-1-338-09881-5

Printed in China   38
First edition, September 2018

Book design by Kathleen Westray

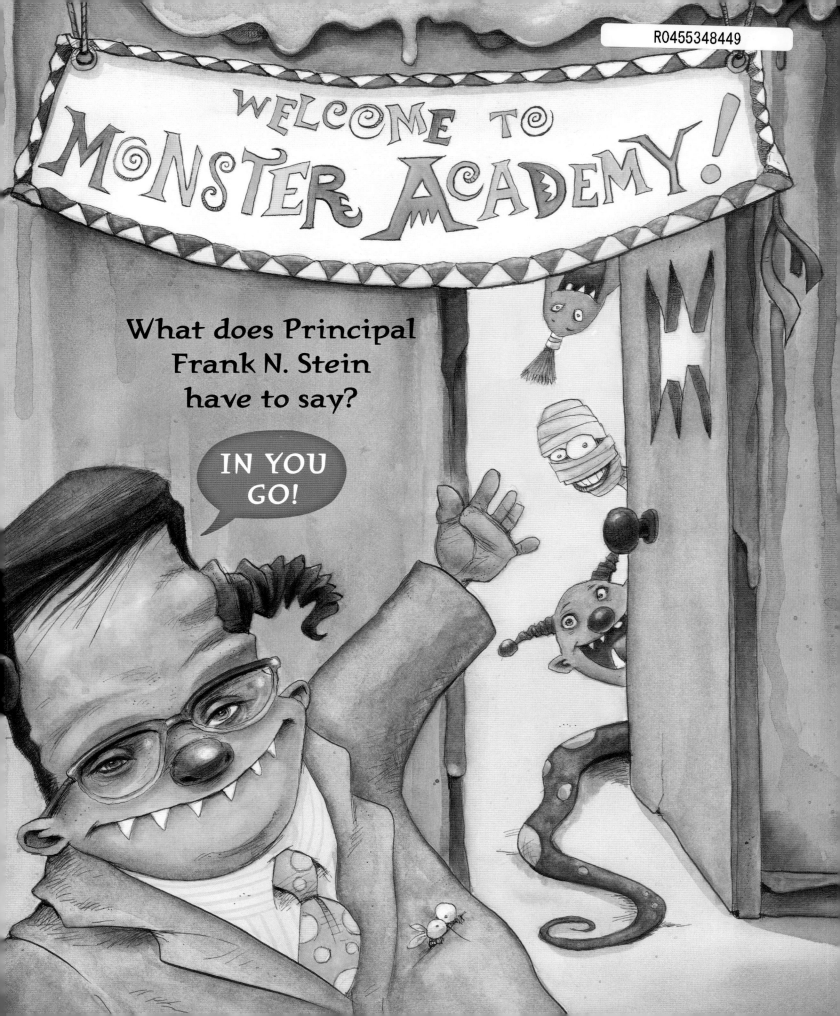

"Hello, monsters! Come on in.
When everyone's here, class will begin."

"Miss Mummy! So many bandages!
Did you get hurt?"

Serpentina's snakes HISSSSS.

"I'm not hurt! I'm just old.
I look good for my age, or so I'm told."

"And why do your words rhyme?" asks Bog.

"Every mummy has a curse.
Mine is that I speak in verse.
But it could be worse!
I could . . .

SCREAM

when I converse."

But are little monsters
scared of screams?

NO!

They scream
right back.

ARRRRRRRGH!

"I count: Yeti, Yoti, Fifi, Spec,
Serpentina, Vic, Bog . . . wait!
That's seven when we should have eight.
Is our newest monster late?"

CRASH!

"It's our new student!
Here we go!
You must be
Tornado Jo!"

ZAZOOM!

But Jo shouts:
"NO!"

"Say hello!" the students yell.

"NO!" says Jo, spinning
into Vic's lunchbox.

"NO!" says Jo, knocking
over Bog's chair.

"NO!" says Jo,
bumping into Spec.

"NO!" says Jo, yanking
Serpentina's snakes.

"NO!" says Jo, kicking
the table near Yeti and Yoti.

"NO!" says Tornado Jo.
"NO! NO! NO!"

"Jo is the **WORST MONSTER EVER!**" yips Fifi.
"Make Tornado Jo stop!"

"We're all monsters, Fifi dear.
Jo will learn some manners here."

NO!
NO! NO!
NO!

Tornado Jo
spins and spins and spins
until . . .

UMMPF!

Jo lands on the floor.

"Now get up, Jo!
It's time for math.
Count your missing teeth —
for our Monster Tooth Graph!"

Poor Vampire Vic!
He wiggles his big, scary fang.
He doesn't want to say
ZERO.

"How about you, Jo? Missing teeth?
Any above? Any beneath?"

"NO!" says Jo.

But Jo *is* missing a tooth.
Miss Mummy writes it down.

"Now, quick —
how about you, Vic?"

Vic jiggles his loose fang.

"ZERO," he says. He almost cries.

MISSING TEETH							
Fifi							
Spec							1
Serpentina							3
Bog							1
Yeti							2
Yoti							2
Vic							2
Jo							1
TOTAL							12

"Add up the teeth.
Twelve, you say?
Good job! We'll go
to the Lab today!"

YAY!

And what do you think
little monsters build at
Monster Maker's Lab?

A Creepy Castle!

Everybody helps,
even the class bats.
Everybody but Jo.

"Come on, Jo!"
Serpentina yells.
"It's fun."

Her snakes

HISSSSS.

But Jo says: "NO!"

Now it's almost lunchtime.

Wiggle, wiggle, wiggle.
Vic pulls his fang.
It won't come out!

Vic is so unhappy, he doesn't care when Jo grabs his blood orange and gives him a big, juicy apple.

Does Jo want to be friends? Maybe!

Crunch, crunch, crunch.

Vic takes three big bites.

"Want some?"
he asks Jo.

"NO!"
says Jo.

Time for Monster Recess! Run to the Swamp Pool!
But only Vic goes in—all alone.

"Help me make a swamp monster?" Vic asks Jo.

"NO!" says Jo.

Tornado Jo stomps and
kicks swamp stink at Vic.
It splatters on everyone.

"You are the **WORST MONSTER EVER!**" says Fifi.

And then she looks at Vic and

HOWLS!

"Your fang is gone!"

"Where is it?" Bog asks. "You need it for the Tooth Troll!"

"Help me find it!" cries Vic. **"PLEASE!"**

Everyone shouts:
"YES!"

But Jo says:
"NO!"

Spec, Bog,
and the twins
search high.

No fang.

Serpentina,
Fifi, and Vic
search low.

No fang.

Miss Mummy checks the Swamp Pool.

No fang.

"Please help, Jo!" says Vic.

"NO! NO! NO!"

Tornado Jo begins to spin . . .

. . . and spin . . . and spin . . . and spin!

WHOOSH!

One final spin, and Jo falls over.

"You're a HUMAN?" screams Vic.

"NO!" shouts Jo. "I'm a MONSTER!"

"HELP!" Vic yells. "There's a HUMAN in our class!"

What happens when monster children see a human?

MONSTERS RUN!

Back inside, Miss Mummy calms them down.

"Jo is a human and a monster, too. She belongs in class, just like each of you."

How can she be both?

"I get it!" says Vic. "We're scary,
but so is she!"

"So Tornado Jo is one of US!" they howl.

Vic gives a big, gap-fanged smile.

"We couldn't find my tooth, Miss Mummy.
But it still counts as **ONE**! I'm
not a **ZERO** anymore!"

Everyone cheers.
Even Miss Mummy.
She writes a big number **ONE**
next to Vic's name.

"Miss Mummy," says Fifi,
"now we can change the total
from twelve to thirteen!"

The perfect
monster
number!

MISSING TEETH

Name						Total
Fifi						1
Spec						3
Serpentina						1
Bog						2
Yeti						2
Yoti						2
Vic						1
Jo						1

TOTAL **13**

The school bell rings.
Time for monsters to go home.

Principal Frank N. Stein asks,
"How was the new monster today?"

"She's the **WORST MONSTER EVER!**"
the class shouts.

This time Jo smiles.

"Our little Jo?
Let's just say
Jo's starting to learn
our monster way.
Sometimes it's hard
when you begin.
But now I think . . .
she'll fit right in."

Before they leave,
Jo points.

"My tooth!" Vic yells.
"Ernie has it! Thanks, Jo!
See you tomorrow?"

"YES!" says Jo.
"YES, YOU WILL!"

Class Pet
ERNIE